Happy Birthday Porter!

Love, Daphne + Alex

MY FIRST
Raggedy

Ann

Raggedy Ann and the Birthday Surprise

BY STEPHANIE TRUE PETERS

ILLUSTRATED BY KATHRYN MITTER

BASED ON CHARACTERS CREATED
BY JOHNNY GRUELLE

SIMON & SCHUSTER BOOKS FOR YOUNG READERS

SIMON & SCHUSTER BOOKS FOR YOUNG READERS

An imprint of Simon & Schuster Children's Publishing Division

1230 Avenue of the Americas, New York, New York 10020

Book design by Lily Malcom

The text for this book is set in Adobe Jenson.

The illustrations are rendered in watercolor and ink.

Printed in Hong Kong

10 9 8 7 6 5 4 3 2 1

Library of Congress Cataloging-in-Publication Data

Peters, Stephanie True, 1965-

My first Raggedy Ann : Raggedy Ann and the birthday surprise /

by Stephanie True Peters ; illustrated by Kathryn Mitter.

        p.   cm.

"Based on characters created by Johnny Gruelle."

Summary: Raggedy Ann plans some special surprises for Raggedy Andy's birthday,

including a red balloon that carries him up into the sky and off to an adventure.

ISBN 0-689-83136-6

[1. Birthdays Fiction. 2. Balloons Fiction. 3. Parties Fiction. 4. Dolls Fiction.] I. Mitter, Kathryn, ill. II. Title.

PZ7.P441835Mt 2000

[E]—dc21

99-24899

CIP

The History of Raggedy Ann

One day, a little girl named Marcella discovered an old rag doll in her attic. Because Marcella was often ill and had to spend much of her time at home, her father, a writer named Johnny Gruelle, looked for ways to keep her entertained. He was inspired by Marcella's rag doll, which had bright shoe-button eyes and red yarn hair. The doll became known as Raggedy Ann.

Knowing how much Marcella adored Raggedy Ann, Johnny Gruelle wrote stories about the doll. He later collected the stories he had written for Marcella and published them in a series of books. He gave Raggedy Ann a brother, Raggedy Andy, and over the years the two rag dolls acquired many friends.

Raggedy Ann has been an important part of Americana for more than half a century, as well as a treasured friend to many generations of readers. After all, she is much more than a rag doll—she is a symbol of caring and love, of compassion and generosity. Her magical world is one that promises to delight children of all ages for years to come.

One beautiful sunny morning, Raggedy Ann carried a big white box out of the playhouse. Raggedy Andy tagged along after her.

"What's in the box?" Raggedy Andy asked her, his shoe-button eyes bright with curiosity.

"Never you mind what's in here," Raggedy Ann said. She headed down the meadow path. Raggedy Andy followed.

"It looks heavy," Raggedy Andy said. "Would you like me to carry it for you?" He tried to take the box from her.

"Please, Raggedy Andy, don't touch this box!" Raggedy Ann exclaimed. Raggedy Andy put his hands behind his back.

Just then, Fido came charging down the path.

"Raggedy Ann, come quickly!" he barked. "Babette has torn her silk dress!"

"Oh my!" Raggedy Ann cried. She set the box down and hurried back to the playhouse as fast as her cotton legs could carry her. Fido followed at her heels.

Raggedy Andy stayed behind. He couldn't take his eyes off the box.

What could be in there? Raggedy Andy wondered. He walked around and around the box, but couldn't find a clue.

He lifted the box. It was as light as a cloud, but it wasn't empty. Something thumped inside it.

He looked back toward the playhouse. "Surely Raggedy Ann won't mind if I take just one little peek."

Slowly he lifted the lid . . .

. . . and out popped a big red balloon tied with a bright blue ribbon! Raggedy Andy was so surprised, he dropped the box lid. The red balloon flew to the sky.

"Oh no!" he exclaimed. He jumped up and caught the end of the ribbon. But the balloon was very big, and Raggedy Andy's cotton-stuffed body was very light. Instead of Raggedy Andy pulling the balloon back to the ground, the balloon pulled Raggedy Andy up into the air!

"Oh my, oh my!" Raggedy Andy cried. "Help!" But there was no one around.

No one, that is, except Mr. Sparrow. Mr. Sparrow had been watching
Raggedy Andy the whole time. When he saw Raggedy Andy soar into
the sky, he flew as fast as he could to the playhouse.

"Raggedy Ann!" Mr. Sparrow chirped at the window. "Raggedy Andy
is floating away!"

Raggedy Ann clapped her rag hands. "I knew he'd open that box!"
she cried happily. "Now we shall have plenty of time to get his special
surprise ready." Babette, whose dress wasn't torn at all, cheered. So did
the other dolls from the nursery.

"Mr. Sparrow, will you keep an eye on Raggedy Andy?" Raggedy Ann asked. "When the sun is overhead, please bring him back to the playhouse." Mr. Sparrow chirped again and flew off to follow Raggedy Andy.

High above the treetops, Raggedy Andy dangled at the end of the
ribbon. He wasn't afraid. His soft cotton body wouldn't get hurt even if
he fell from a great height.

"Whee!" he shouted. "I'm flying!" He marveled at the ground below.
"Everything in the meadow seems so different from up here."

Suddenly, he saw something very strange. "Why, what's that? It looks
like a flower, but it's not like any flower I've ever seen growing in the
meadow. And it's—it's hopping!"

From the ground, Grandpa Hoppytoad heard Raggedy Andy. But he didn't want to ruin the special surprise Raggedy Ann had planned for Raggedy Andy. So instead of stopping to talk to Raggedy Andy, he hopped faster to the playhouse with the present he was carrying.

A big gust of wind blew Raggedy Andy around and around in dizzying circles. When he stopped spinning, he couldn't see the hopping flower anymore. Instead, he saw dozens of twinkling lights on the meadow path.

Are those tiny puddles? Raggedy Andy wondered. *But it hasn't rained in days. What could they be?*

One by one, the meadow folk flew toward the playhouse. Each held
a tiny bottle of something good to drink.

"I'm so excited," squeaked the youngest fairy, nearly dropping her
bottle. "Won't Raggedy Andy like his special surprise?"

"Shhh!" the oldest fairy whispered. "He's right above us. Quick,
everyone! Hide!" And with a tinkle of laughter, they all flew into the
tall grass.

"The lights have vanished!" Raggedy Andy cried in surprise. Then he spied something else just as puzzling. It was round with many colorful patches, and moved very, very slowly.

"If I didn't know any better," Raggedy Andy said, laughing, "I'd say that Mrs. Turtle had painted her shell! But she would never do that, for then she couldn't pretend to be a rock when she slept. But if it's not Mrs. Turtle, what can it be?"

Mrs. Turtle listened to Raggedy Andy and smiled. With a tray of cookies balanced on her back, she carefully plodded on to the playhouse. The sweets were Raggedy Andy's favorites, and she didn't want to drop any of them.

He's sure to be hungry after his adventures in the clouds, she thought.

Raggedy Andy *was* hungry. The sun was high overhead, and he was ready to go back to the playhouse to have some lunch.

"But how will I get down?" he said sadly. "I can't just let go of the balloon."

"If you like," came a voice behind him, "I can pop your big red balloon with my sharp beak."

Raggedy Andy spun around.

There was Mr. Sparrow—and he was about to prick the balloon!

"No! Stop!" Raggedy Andy shouted. "This isn't my balloon!"

Mr. Sparrow cocked his head. "Not your balloon?"

Raggedy Andy hung his head. "No, it's Raggedy Ann's balloon. Please, won't you help me get it back to her?"

"It is a very big balloon, but I'll try." Mr. Sparrow gripped Raggedy Andy's feet with his own feet and, with a flurry of wings, started to pull.

Mr. Sparrow, Raggedy Andy, and the balloon flew back toward the meadow. But instead of returning to the box on the path, Mr. Sparrow tugged Raggedy Andy straight to the playhouse. Still holding on to Raggedy Andy's feet, Mr. Sparrow knocked on the door with his sharp beak.

"Raggedy Ann, are you there?" he called. "I've brought Raggedy Andy with me!"

"Well, bring him in," Raggedy Ann said. And she opened the door.
The playhouse was dark. Mr. Sparrow pulled Raggedy Andy and the
balloon inside.

"Raggedy Ann, where are you?" Raggedy Andy whispered.

Suddenly, the room was ablaze with light.

"Happy birthday!" shouted a dozen voices.

Raggedy Andy was so surprised, he let go of the balloon and fell to the ground with a soft *thump*.

"My birthday!" he exclaimed. "I'd forgotten it was my birthday today!"

Raggedy Ann and their friends from the meadow and the nursery laughed. "Well, we didn't! We have all kinds of good things to eat and drink here. And when your tummy's full, you can open your presents." She looked up at the big red balloon floating on the ceiling. "But I see you've already opened the one I got you!" Her black eyes twinkled merrily.

Raggedy Andy gave Raggedy Ann a warm hug. Then he jumped as high as he could and caught hold of the blue ribbon again. This is the best birthday ever!" he called, swinging his legs back and forth. "I can't wait to take my birthday balloon out for another adventure tomorrow!"